CONGO
THE SEARCH FOR ZINJ

By Jim Thomas
Based on the movie *Congo*
Illustrated by Uldis Klavins

A Random House PICTUREBACK®

Random House 🏠 New York

Copyright © 1995 by Paramount Pictures.
All rights reserved under International and Pan-American Copyright Conventions. Published in the United States by Random House, Inc., New York, and simultaneously in Canada by Random House of Canada Limited, Toronto.
Library of Congress Catalog Card Number: 94-73865

ISBN: 0-679-87592-1
Manufactured in the United States of America 10 9 8 7 6 5 4 3 2 1
Random House, Inc. New York, Toronto, London, Sydney, Auckland

Monroe Kelly was leading an expedition into Africa. A search was on for a rare kind of diamond used in space satellites. According to legend, the lost city of Zinj was rich with these special diamonds. Monroe's team had just parachuted into the Congo jungle to search for the ancient, mysterious city.

One of the team members bounded over toward Monroe.
She was a 130-pound gorilla!

"Amy!" Monroe said, laughing.

Amy jumped up and gave him a hug, then ran back toward
Professor Peter Elliot.

Peter had raised Amy and taught her sign language. By using a special glove that translated her hand gestures into sounds, Amy could actually talk!

"Amy good gorilla!" she said to Peter.

"Yes, you are," Peter said. "Where's Karen?"

"Right here," said Dr. Karen Ross, joining the group.

Together, they looked down the trail.

Long ago, three dead trees had collapsed toward each other to form a huge natural gate. Through it, the group could see where their path led: into the darkest, deepest part of the forest.

Monroe signaled to the porters, who were along to help carry supplies. He adjusted his backpack and said, "Let's go."

By late afternoon, the team had reached Lake Ragora. On the far shore they could see Mount Mukenko. Somewhere on the other side of that volcano lay Zinj.

After blowing up their inflatable boats, the group set out across the lake.

Halfway across, the front of the first boat lifted and dropped violently. "What was that?" Karen asked.

"Hippo!" yelled Monroe, rowing hard. Hippos were very dangerous and often attacked boats.

Then the side of the boat lifted up. When it dropped back down, Monroe found himself staring into the hippo's gaping jaws!

With a roar, the hippo slashed at the boat. The beast's sharp tusks punctured it easily.

Monroe and Peter rowed frantically for shore as their boat deflated underneath them.

Finally, the three explorers pulled themselves onto dry land—
they were exhausted and wet, but safe.

The next day, the group entered a passageway on the slopes of Mount Mukenko that would take them through the volcano. It was very hot inside, with deadly gases and fumes making it hard to breathe. Far below, the explorers could see bubbling molten rock.

After they finally came out into daylight and clean air, Karen said, "I don't know where to go from here. It's up to Amy now."

Amy had been born in this area. The team was counting on her to remember where Zinj was.

Peter could tell that Amy was excited to be back. She ran toward the forest, saying, "Amy go this way! Peter go this way!"

Amy led them down the side of Mukenko, through the jungle to a gold-colored stream.

When she saw the stream, Karen cried, "Amy's done it! A golden stream is supposed to lead to the city!"

Amy looked proud. "Amy good gorilla!" she said.

The group followed the stream through a fissure in a nearby rock wall. There they found...

The lost city of Zinj!

The team walked through the city in a daze.

"The first settlers found the diamonds," Karen said, "then they built the city around the mine to protect it. It's said that their guards attacked strangers on sight."

Peter stopped. "But where's the mine?" he asked. "It looks like we're at a dead end." The team had walked into a walled courtyard with no exits but the way they had come in.

That's when they heard strange wheezing and growling sounds coming from behind them.

The explorers turned to find the entrance of the courtyard blocked by a group of snarling, gray, gorilla-like creatures.

"We're trapped!" Monroe said.

"They look like some kind of mutant gorillas," said Peter.

Suddenly the gray gorillas fell quiet and cocked their heads, as if listening. After a moment, they began to withdraw.

Amy tugged at Peter's sleeve. "Earth bad, Peter. Earth bad."

Monroe looked over. "What's she mean?"

Monroe got his answer as an earthquake rocked the city, knocking the group to the ground. Mukenko was erupting!

"We've got to get out of here!" Monroe said, struggling to his feet. But he fell again as the courtyard floor began to tilt.

Suddenly the team members found themselves sliding through a jagged crack in the floor!

With a *thud*, they landed in a dark corridor.

Monroe sat up and shook his head. "Is everyone okay?" he asked.

"I'm all right," Karen said, standing up. She looked down the hallway at Peter and Amy. They were in front of one of the walls, staring at a mural painted there.

"Peter?" asked Karen.

"Come over here and bring a light," Peter said. "I think I've found something."

The mural Peter had found showed a nobleman commanding a gray gorilla to attack a thief.

Peter studied the painting closely. "Now I understand," he said. "The gray gorillas were trained to attack anyone who came to the city to steal diamonds. The gray gorillas are the *guards*!"

The group continued along the corridor before turning a corner into daylight. They were standing at the bottom of a large crater. The dirt walls and floor glinted strangely.

Karen picked up something from the dirt. When she turned back to the group, she held an enormous diamond in her hand!

"We've found the mine!" she said.

Suddenly they heard wheezing and growling again.

"Uh-oh," Peter said.

The group watched as dozens of gray gorillas emerged from an arch in the wall above them. More and more surrounded the team, until there were too many to count.

Monroe raised his rifle. "We're in trouble," he said.

Then, without warning, Mukenko erupted again. The force of the blast sent everyone sprawling, including the gorillas.

Monroe grabbed Peter by the shirt collar as a crack opened in the ground beneath him, jetting hot steam. Out of the crack a huge spike of stone was forced. When it stopped moving, it reached all the way up to the lip of the crater, forming a bridge between the group and the jungle above.

"Go!" Monroe yelled, pushing Peter toward the spike. "We'll climb out!"

But before Peter could even touch the stone bridge, he was clubbed to the ground. He looked up to see a gray gorilla clinging to the spike, snarling down at them.

Suddenly a voice cried out, "Bad gorilla! Ugly! Amy say, Go away!" Peter turned to see Amy charging at the much larger animal.

The gray was confused at the sight of this talking gorilla. Ducking its head, it jumped off the spike, away from the team.

Amy cradled Peter in her arms and tenderly touched his face. "Peter," she moaned.

"I'm okay, Amy," Peter said. "Thank you."

Monroe looked back at them as he helped Karen up onto the spike. "Let's go! Hurry!"

The group ran past the golden stream, climbed a high hill, and looked back. Lava was slowly covering the city.

Karen pulled out the diamond she had brought with her. In her hand was the only evidence that Zinj had ever existed. Now the lost city was truly lost.

Karen looked at her companions' weary faces. She smiled. Together, they'd come through it all in one piece.

Amy picked a flower and handed it to Peter. Then she disappeared into the trees.

"Where's she going?" Karen asked.

"This is where she belongs," Peter said. "She's going home."

Monroe clapped Peter on the shoulder. "It's time for us to go, too."

They took one last look at the burning city, then turned to begin the long journey home.